J FLORENCE
Florence, Debbi Michiko,
Apple and Annie, the hamster duo /

My Furry Foster Family

Apple and Annie, the Hamster Duo

by Debbi Michiko Florence

illustrated by Melanie Demmer

PICTURE WINDOW BOOKS
a capstone imprint

To my aunt, Toshie Hatami, the best hamster mom! — DMF

My Furry Foster Family is published by
Picture Window Books, a Capstone imprint
1710 Roe Crest Drive, North Mankato, Minnesota 56003
www.capstonepub.com

Library of Congress Cataloging-in-Publication Data
Names: Florence, Debbi Michiko, author.
Title: Apple and Annie, the hamster duo / by Debbi Michiko Florence.
Description: North Mankato, Minnesota : Capstone Press, [2020] | Series:
My furry foster family | Audience: Age 5–7. | Audience: K to Grade 3.
Identifiers: LCCN 2019004135| ISBN 9781515844730 (library binding) |
ISBN 9781515845614 (paperback) | ISBN 9781515844778 (eBook PDF)
Subjects: LCSH: Hamsters as pets—Anecdotes—Juvenile literature. |
Foster care of animals—Juvenile literature.
Classification: LCC SF459.H3 F56 2020 | DDC 636.935/6—dc23
LC record available at https://lccn.loc.gov/2019004135

Designer: Lori Bye

Photo Credits: Mari Bolte, 66, 69; Melanie Demmer, 71; Roy Thomas, 70

Printed in the United States of America.
PA70

Table of Contents

Dad
(Tim Takano)

Mom
(Cindy Takano)

Me
(Kaita Takano)

Eraser

Ollie

Hannah Miller,
my best friend

Joss Lawrence,
Happy Tails
Rescue

CHAPTER 1

The Long Wait

I love lots of things. I love my family, my dog, and my best friend, Hannah, most of all. When we're all together, I am one happy kid.

Last Tuesday Hannah came home with me and my mom after school. Ollie, my mini dachshund, greeted us loudly when we walked in the kitchen door. *Yip! Yip! Yip!*

Mom opened the refrigerator and asked, "Girls, how about a snack?"

"No, thank you, Mrs. Takano," Hannah said.

I smiled. I was glad to hear that. Hannah and I had plans. It was a special day. I didn't want to waste time eating snacks, even though I really like snack time!

"I bet Ollie would like a snack," Hannah said. "Can I give him one?"

"Sure!" Mom said.

Hannah reached into a jar on the counter. Ollie wagged his tail. He knew what was in that jar.

"Ollie, sit!" Hannah said. She held up a dog cookie.

Ollie sat.

"Good boy!" Hannah said. She tossed the treat, and Ollie caught it in mid-air.

Hannah and I went into the living room. We sat on the couch and looked out the window. We were waiting for a special visitor.

"What time is Joss coming?" Hannah asked.

"I don't know," I said, bouncing on the couch. "I can't wait to see the new pets she's bringing. They're going to be so cool!"

Joss is a lady who works for Happy Tails Rescue. It's a wonderful place that helps homeless animals. Last year my family adopted Ollie from Happy Tails. Now we foster pets for them. That means we take care of animals until they find a forever home.

"What are you getting this time?" Hannah asked. "A bird? Maybe more kittens?"

I shook my head. "Two dwarf hamsters! They're sisters!" I said.

"Hamsters!" Hannah squealed. "Awesome!"

Sometimes Hannah comes to the pet store with me to buy Ollie's dog food. We always stop to look at the animals, especially the furry ones. We like watching the hamsters. They look so cute, running on their exercise wheels.

"Do you know how to take care of hamsters?" Hannah asked. "They're probably going to be a lot different from Ollie."

I nodded. "Mom found a book about hamsters for me at the bookstore," I said. "It's so great she works there. I read the book three times already."

Hannah and I looked out the window again. I hoped Joss' truck would pull into the driveway soon. Waiting was hard.

I petted Ollie. Hannah petted Ollie. Then Ollie fell asleep.

"You are so lucky to have a dog," Hannah said.

"You can play with Ollie anytime you want," I said.

"Thank you, Kaita," Hannah said with a smile.

I looked out the window yet again.

Mom walked into the living room. She wore her straw hat. She always wore it when she worked in the garden. "Are you girls just sitting here, looking out the window?" she asked.

"We're waiting for Joss," I said.

"You can help in the garden, if you'd like," Mom said. "How about working on a puzzle? Time will seem to go faster."

"A puzzle would be good. It *is* a little boring to wait," Hannah said. She gave a little smile and patted my shoulder. "Sorry, Kaita."

"That's OK," I said. "I'm a little bored too."

I grabbed a puzzle box off the shelf. Hannah and I sat on the floor by the coffee table and dumped out the pieces. The puzzle was a picture of ocean animals. Brightly colored fish, a sea turtle, and a dolphin swam in the water.

Hannah and I picked through the pile. We looked for edge pieces first. Then we slowly started to put those pieces together. I love the happy clicking sound puzzle pieces make when they fit! Soon we had the entire edge done.

Without warning Ollie woke up and ran to the front door. *Yip! Yip! Yip!*

"Joss is here!" Mom said, coming in from the garden.

I looked at the clock. An hour had flown by! Mom was right. Doing the puzzle had kept us busy.

Mom picked up Ollie and opened the door.

"Hello, Takano family!" Joss said. "Hello, Hannah!"

Ollie wagged his tail and wiggled in Mom's arms.

"Yes, hello to you too, Ollie!" Joss said.

Ollie liked Joss. A lot! Joss had fostered Ollie while he was waiting for his forever family—US!

Joss carried a big plastic container. It looked like one of the tubs Mom kept my old schoolwork in. This one was bigger, though, without a lid.

Our new foster animals were finally here!

I leaned in to look. Bubbles of excitement tickled my tummy.

Then the bubbles popped.

I didn't see any hamsters inside the plastic tub. Where were they?

CHAPTER 2

Meet Apple and Annie

I looked at Joss. "Did you forget the hamsters?" I asked. I hoped she hadn't. I didn't want to wait any longer!

"No, Kaita," Joss said with a smile. "Apple and Annie are in the little box inside this tub."

I looked again. I saw a box with air holes. I heard scratching sounds coming from inside it.

"We need to keep the hamsters in a room away from Ollie," Joss said. "I know he wouldn't hurt them on purpose, but it's better to keep the pets apart."

Mom led Joss to our guest room. It's a small room that my dad sometimes uses as his studio. Dad is a graphic artist. He makes things like ads and logos. Sometimes Dad and I draw pictures together.

Joss put the tub on top of a table. "The hamsters won't be able to climb up the sides of the tub," she said. "To be safe, though, always keep the door to this room closed."

"Cool," I said, looking closely inside. "It looks like a mini playground."

"It does!" Hannah said, peering over my shoulder.

In the center of the tub was a red exercise wheel. A yellow plastic tube lay beside it. The hamsters could run on the wheel and race through the tube. I wished I were a hamster so I could play in there!

The tub also held a water bottle and a green dish filled with seeds. Litter covered the bottom of the tub. It looked like tiny balls of brown paper.

"Ready to meet Apple and Annie?" Joss asked.

"Ready!" Hannah and I said.

Joss opened the box. Out climbed two fuzzy, tan-and-white hamsters.

"Cute!" I said. I smiled so big my cheeks hurt.

"Apple and Annie lived together with a nice family. Sadly one of the kids had allergies. Whenever he was near the hamsters, he sneezed and coughed. So now Apple and Annie need a new home."

"Which one is which?" Hannah asked. The hamsters looked alike.

Joss pointed to one of them. "See that spot that looks like a crooked apple? That's Apple!" she said.

"Can I hold her?" I asked.

"Yes, of course," Joss said. "In fact I hope you play with both hamsters a lot. They get used to being touched, and that makes them better pets."

Joss scooped up Apple and put her in my hands. I giggled.

"She's so soft," I said.

I cupped my hands so Apple wouldn't get away. Then I lifted her to my face. We were nose to nose. Apple wiggled her whiskers. She was adorable!

"Would you like to hold Annie?" Joss asked Hannah.

Hannah nodded, and Joss put Annie in her hands. Now each of us had a hamster to play with.

After a few minutes, Joss wished us luck and said goodbye. Apple started to crawl up my arm. Annie squirmed in Hannah's hands. The hamsters' little feet tickled. I didn't want our new foster pets to escape, so Hannah and I put them back in the tub.

We watched the hamsters play for a while. Apple ran on the exercise wheel. Annie stuffed seeds into her mouth. Her cheeks puffed out like balloons. Hannah and I laughed.

After Apple got off the wheel, she ran through the tunnel a few times. So did Annie. Then they made a nest with the litter. They curled up next to each other and fell asleep.

"They sure didn't play very long," Hannah said. "Do you think they're bored? Like we were, waiting for Joss?"

"I'm not sure," I said. "Mom said hamsters are nocturnal. They sleep a lot during the day and move around at night. I guess that's why Mom and Dad put them here in the guest room. They didn't want the hamsters to keep us awake while we were trying to sleep."

"OK. So maybe they *aren't* bored," Hannah said.

"Maybe they aren't," I said. I looked at the wheel and the tunnel. I knew what it felt like to not have enough fun stuff to do. "I have an idea. Come on! Let's go to my room!"

CHAPTER 3

Time for Toys

Hannah and I sat down on my bedroom floor. Ollie came running in, wagging his tail.

"Did you miss us, Ollie?" I asked. I gave him a big hug. Hannah rubbed his muzzle. "I'm sorry you couldn't meet Apple and Annie. I think you'd make a good big brother!"

"So what's your idea, Kaita?" Hannah asked me.

"Let's make toys for Apple and Annie," I said.

Hannah smiled. "Yes! That sounds like fun!" she said.

I grabbed the hamster book Mom had gotten for me. Then I dragged out my art supply box from the closet. Ollie stuck his head in the box. He pulled out a cardboard tube and started chewing on it.

"This book has some good projects in it," I said. "I marked the best ones."

We flipped through the book and quickly got to work. Hannah made a house out of a square box. She cut out a door and windows. She called it the Hamster Hut.

I took two empty toilet-paper rolls and cut them in half. I taped the four short tubes to a piece of cardboard. "Look, Hannah," I said. "I made a stage for them to climb on."

"Great!" she said.

With the leftover cardboard, we made a ramp.

When we were done making the toys, we checked on Apple and Annie. They were awake!

"Hello, Apple! Hello, Annie!" I said. "Look! We made you two some toys."

Hannah placed the house on one side of the tub. I put the stage on the other side and set up the ramp over the tunnel. Then Hannah and I sat back and watched.

Apple scurried to Hannah's Hamster Hut right away. She peeked in one of the windows. After a few seconds, she went inside.

"She likes it!" Hannah said.

Annie climbed over the ramp, back and forth. Neither hamster seemed to see my stage. I felt a little sad about that. How could I get Apple and Annie to play on it?

I ran to the kitchen. Mom was making dinner. "Can I please have a few carrot slices?" I asked.

Mom raised an eyebrow. She wasn't sure what I needed the carrots for. She cut a few slices for me anyway.

"Thanks!" I called, running back to the guest room.

I put the carrots on top of the stage. Apple sniffed the air. Then she and Annie followed their noses to the stage. Apple put her front paws on the cardboard and stretched. With a hop she was on top! Annie hopped up too! The hamsters nibbled their treats. They looked so sweet holding the carrots in their paws.

"Great idea, Kaita," Hannah said.

Apple and Annie looked very happy. Hannah and I watched them play with their new toys until Hannah's mom picked her up for dinner.

***

Yip! Yip! Yip! Ollie ran to the back door. Dad was home from work.

"Dad! Come meet Apple and Annie! They are so tiny and cute! Hurry!" I said. I grabbed his arm and pulled.

"Let me get my shoes off first, Kaita," Dad said with a laugh.

I pulled Dad toward the guest room. I talked nonstop the whole way to the hamsters' tub.

"Joss said to keep the door closed," I said. "She worried Ollie might bother the hamsters. I think he'd be nice, though. Don't you? He's a good boy."

"Yes, he is," Dad said. He looked into the tub. "Wow, you were right. They *are* tiny and cute."

Apple was in the house Hannah had made. Annie was running on the wheel.

"They came with the tunnel and wheel. Hannah and I made the other toys," I said proudly.

Dad nodded. "I'm sure Apple and Annie are thankful for the gifts," he said.

After we ate dinner, Mom went to work. Dad and I finished the puzzle that Hannah and I had started. Ollie snored on the couch.

"Nice job!" Dad said as we looked at the ocean picture.

"You too, Dad," I said. "Is it OK if I play with Apple and Annie before bedtime? Joss said we should play with them a lot."

"Sure. Go ahead," he said.

I skipped to the guest room and looked in the tub. Apple was running on the wheel. *Squeak! Squeak! Squeak!* I peeked in the house but didn't see Annie.

"Well, where—" I started to say.

I heard a small scratching sound nearby. I looked around.

Annie was on the table, outside the tub!

"Annie, what are you doing out here?" I said, scooping her up. "How did you get out?"

I petted Annie's head with my finger. I was glad I had come to check on the hamsters when I did. Thankfully they were safe.

I put Annie back in the tub with
her sister. They greeted each other
with a nose kiss.

I wondered how Annie had gotten
out. The sides of the tub were tall
and slippery.

I told myself it was probably a one-time thing. I was sure it wouldn't happen again.

"Good night, Apple. Good night, Annie. I'm really glad you're here," I said. I turned out the light and went to my room.

CHAPTER 4

The Great Escape

The next morning I helped Dad make our special Saturday waffles. He cracked the eggs. I measured the flour, sugar, and milk. I mixed. Then Dad scooped the batter into the waffle iron.

Breakfast was ready by the time Mom got back from her run. The waffles were delicious!

Mom went to work after breakfast. I cleaned Apple and Annie's tub. I gave them fresh seeds and water.

Once the hamsters were taken care of, Dad and I took Ollie to the dog park. Ollie got to play off his leash there with the other dogs.

Our neighbor Mrs. Ahmed and her dog, Lucy, were already there. Lucy was a beagle. She and Ollie liked to chase each other.

"Hello, Kaita! Hello, Tim!" Mrs. Ahmed said. "How are you today?"

"We're great, Mrs. Ahmed!" I said.

"Are you still fostering all of those kittens?" she asked. "I think it's wonderful that you open your home to so many pets in need."

"No, all of the kittens found their forever families," I said. "We got two foster hamsters yesterday. Dwarf hamsters! They're sisters! They fit right in your hand. Would you like to adopt them?"

Mrs. Ahmed smiled. "I don't think Lucy would like that very much, Kaita," she said. "I hope you find a good home for them."

"Thank you, Badia," Dad said. "I'm sure we will."

Mrs. Ahmed got me thinking. I wondered what the perfect place for Apple and Annie would be. I asked Dad on the walk home.

"I talked to Joss about that," Dad said. "Hamsters need a house that's not too busy. They should get lots of playtime and attention. They're better pets for older kids or adults. Little kids don't always know how to be gentle. Hamsters are tiny, fragile animals, you know."

I nodded. "Holding a hamster is kind of like holding a soap bubble."

"Right," Dad said.

"Apple and Annie need to be adopted out together too," I said. "It wouldn't be right to break apart two sisters."

"Right again," Dad said. "They're a bonded pair. They need each other."

When we got home, Ollie took a long drink from his water bowl. I gave him a treat.

"Kaita, Mom will be home in an hour. What do you want to do until then?" Dad asked.

I didn't have to think one second about that.

"Play with Apple and Annie!" I said.

"OK," Dad said. "Ollie and I will hang out in the living room."

I went to the guest room and closed the door behind me. "Hi, Apple. Hi, Annie," I said, walking over to the tub.

The hamsters weren't running on the wheel. They weren't racing through the tunnel. I didn't see them in Hannah's little house or on my stage either.

My stomach felt wobbly. So did my head.

They must've buried themselves in the litter. I stuck my hand in. I felt along the bottom of the tub.

No hamsters.

Oh no! What would Joss do if I lost Apple and Annie? Would she stop letting us foster? My hands got sweaty as I crawled on the floor to look for them.

"Dad!" I called. "Come quick!"

"What's wrong?" he asked, hurrying into the room.

"I can't find Apple and Annie! They aren't in their tub!" I chewed my bottom lip, trying not to cry.

Dad got down next to me. "It's OK, Kaita," he said. "Hamsters are great escape artists. They're good at getting out of their cages. Since the door was closed, they have to be in this room somewhere, right?"

"Annie got out yesterday," I said. "I didn't say anything because I didn't think it would happen again."

"We'll find them," Dad said.

I looked under the futon. Dad looked behind his desk. I peeked in the trash can. Dad moved the stacks of paper on the floor.

"Wait," I said. "Do you hear that?"

We got very quiet.

"It sounds like scratching, from behind the bookcase," I said.

Dad carefully moved the bookcase away from the wall. He smiled. "Here they are!" he said.

I crawled over to look. Apple and Annie were calmly chewing on the wood. They looked pretty happy.

Dad picked up Apple. I picked up Annie.

"I'm so glad to see you both," I said.

I kissed the sisters on their tiny heads. Then Dad and I put them back in the tub.

"How do you think they got out?" Dad asked.

I looked at the new toys that Hannah and I had made. My stage was tall. It sat against the side of the tub. "I bet they hopped onto the stage and climbed out," I said.

"I think you're right," Dad said.

I frowned. "I guess I should take out the stage," I said.

"I have a better idea," Dad said. "Take it out for now. After I'm done with my idea, you can put it back in."

"Can I help you?" I asked.

"Of course!" Dad said.

CHAPTER 5

Another Long Wait

Dad and I drove to the hardware store. We bought wood, nails, and a wire screen. Back at home Dad measured, cut, and hammered. I didn't get to help much, but I liked to watch Dad work. Before he was done, I figured out what he was making.

"You're making a top for the tub!" I said.

"Good guess!" Dad said. He held up the cover. The wood frame had a screen to let in air and light. "Let's try this out."

The cover fit perfectly! I put my stage back inside the tub. Apple and Annie were safe in their home, and all of us were very happy about that.

I played with the hamsters every day, as much as I could. Days went by. Weeks went by. No one came to adopt Apple and Annie.

"It can be tough to adopt out hamsters," Mom said to me after talking with Joss. "We have to be patient and keep trying."

I liked having Apple and Annie live with us. I loved playing with them. I didn't mind cleaning their tub. It was easy. Hannah loved to come over and help too. But I really wanted our foster animals to find their forever home.

I got an idea one day. Hannah and I had just finished playing with the hamsters.

"What if we made posters of Apple and Annie?" I asked. "We could put them up at school and the downtown library."

"That's a great idea," Hannah said.

We went to my room and got my art supplies. We made a bunch of colorful posters. Hannah wrote the words. I drew the pictures.

Mom drove us to our school and the library. She even let us put up a poster at her bookstore.

Two days went by. Three days went by. Finally on the fourth day, Joss called.

Mom hung up the phone and smiled. "Good news, Kaita!" she said. "A family will be coming over in a bit to meet Apple and Annie. There are two boys. One is your age. One is a little older. And they have had a hamster before."

"Cool!" I said.

I raced to the front window and waited. Every time a car came up the street, I hoped it would turn into our driveway. It never did. Waiting was super hard!

Then I remembered what Mom had said. If I kept busy, time would seem to move faster. I grabbed a new puzzle off the shelf. This one was a picture of cartoon super heroes.

I dumped the puzzle pieces onto the coffee table. Ollie curled up next to me. One by one I sorted all the edge pieces. Before I could start clicking them together, the doorbell rang.

Yip! Yip! Yip! Ollie ran to the door. Dad, Mom, and I did too.

"Hello!" Dad said, greeting a woman and two boys. "You must be here to see the hamsters."

"Yes, I'm Jill. These are my sons, Evan and Bennett," the woman said.

"Where are the hamsters?" Evan, the older boy, asked.

"I'll show you," I said.

The boys followed me to the guest room. Dad carried Ollie. Mom and Jill came last. It was like a parade!

Mom took the cover off the tub, and Evan put his hand inside. Apple came right over. She sat still as he lifted her up and held her. Bennett reached in next and picked up Annie. Both boys were very careful.

I held my breath. I hoped they would want to adopt the hamsters. Evan stroked Apple's head with a finger. Bennett told Annie how cute she was.

The boys looked at their mom.

"Can we take them home, Mom?" Evan asked.

Jill smiled. "Yes, I think they'll be the perfect fit for our family," she said.

Hooray! Apple and Annie had found their forever home. They had waited a long time for it.

Although I was excited for our next foster pet, I could wait. I was learning how to be much better about waiting. Another foster pet would come soon enough!

Think About It!

1. It's hard for Kaita to wait. What does she do to help pass the time? What are some things you do when you're having a hard time waiting?
2. What would you do if you were Kaita and found Annie outside of her cage the first time?
3. What do Kaita and Hannah like to do when they are together? What do you like to do with your friends?

Draw It! Write It!

1. Make a poster for Apple and Annie to try to find them a forever home. Use words and pictures to get people excited about adopting them.
2. Pretend you are Kaita and write a letter to Evan and Bennett. What would you tell them about Apple and Annie? What tips would you give them?

Glossary

adopt—to take and raise as one's own

bonded—having a close relationship

dachshund—a type of dog with a long body and short legs

dwarf hamster—a tiny, very active rodent with a short tail

foster—to give care and a safe home for a short time

fragile—easily broken or damaged

nocturnal—active at night and resting during the day

patient—calm during difficult times

Author Talk with the Real-Life Kaita

Kaita Takano is a made-up character in this story. There is also a real-life Kaita. Although they share the same first name and a love for fostering pets (and both have a mini dachshund named Ollie), they have some differences. Story Kaita is in third grade. She's Japanese American. Real-Life Kaita is in fifth grade and is half Korean American, half European American.

Debbi Michiko Florence: Kaita, how did you get started fostering?

Kaita: My mom works with other people who foster. She overheard them talking about needing a cat foster and volunteered.

DMF: What was the first pet you fostered?

K: Our first pet was a black cat named Boo. He had a disease called cerebellar hypoplasia. He fell down a lot. I don't remember him much, though, since I was only 6. To me the most memorable pets were the mom cat and her five week-old kittens that we fostered. The mom's name was Sweetie, and the kittens were named Sprinkle, Frosting, Creamsicle, Butterscotch, and Chip. Ollie thought he was their fairy dogfather!

DMF: What do you like best about fostering?

K: That we get to bring in pets who have been abandoned or don't have homes. We get to give them new homes with families who will love them forever.

DMF: What is the biggest challenge?

K: Sometimes the animals get sick, and we can't help them. Other times they stay with us for a long time, and I feel bad because it seems like nobody wants them. But if you wait long enough, the right person will always come along!

DMF: What was your favorite pet that you fostered?

K: Once we fostered two kittens named Sven and Olaf. They were fluffy white babies who loved to snuggle. They were adopted together, which was even better.

DMF: Do you have a special story you'd like to share?

K: Our pony, Angus, came from a place where they didn't take care of their ponies. A friend saved him and fixed his feet, and he came to live with us! It took a long time for him to trust grown-ups, but he liked me right away!

DMF: Do you ever wish you could keep any of the foster pets?

K: All of them!

DMF: Why do you foster instead of keeping the pets?

K: We have kept some, but Dad says we can't keep any more! Fostering is such an easy thing to do. What's one more pet when you already have two? When the animals are in a home instead of a shelter, we can learn more about their personalities before they go to their forever families.

DMF: Is there a pet you haven't fostered yet that you'd like to?

K: Chinchillas! There were some earlier this year for adoption, but my mom said no. (Ollie said yes!)

About the Author

Debbi Michiko Florence writes books for children in her writing studio, The Word Nest. She is an animal lover with a degree in zoology and has worked at a pet store, the Humane Society, a raptor rehabilitation center, and a zoo. She is the author of two chapter book series: Jasmine Toguchi (FSG) and Dorothy & Toto (Picture Window Books). A third-generation Japanese American and a native Californian, Debbi now lives in Connecticut with her husband, a rescue dog, a bunny, and two ducks.

About the Illustrator

Melanie Demmer is an illustrator and designer based out of Los Angeles, California. Originally from Michigan, she graduated with a BFA in illustration from the College for Creative Studies and has been creating artwork for various apparel, animation, and publishing projects ever since. When she isn't making art, Melanie enjoys writing, spending time in the great outdoors, iced tea, scary movies, and taking naps with her cat, Pepper.

Go on all four fun, furry foster adventures!

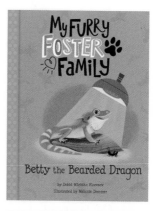

Only from Capstone!